On the Island of Sodor, everyone was getting **excited**. Dowager Hatt was bringing some Very Important Visitors to look around the Island.

"I hope The Fat Controller asks me to show the visitors around!" Thomas puffed.

Gordon sniffed snootily. "**No**, Thomas," he said. "The Fat Controller will ask **me**. I am Gordon and **I** pull the Express."

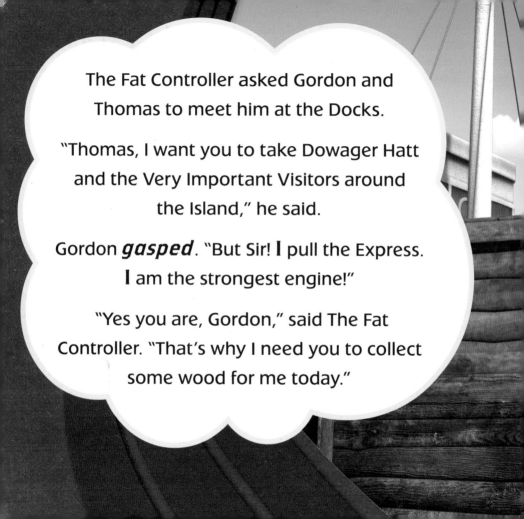

The Fat Controller asked Gordon and Thomas to meet him at the Docks.

"Thomas, I want you to take Dowager Hatt and the Very Important Visitors around the Island," he said.

Gordon *gasped*. "But Sir! I pull the Express. I am the strongest engine!"

"Yes you are, Gordon," said The Fat Controller. "That's why I need you to collect some wood for me today."

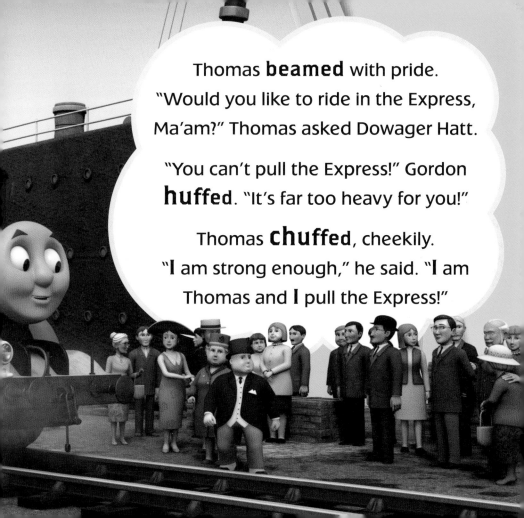

Thomas **beamed** with pride.
"Would you like to ride in the Express, Ma'am?" Thomas asked Dowager Hatt.

"You can't pull the Express!" Gordon **huffed**. "It's far too heavy for you!"

Thomas **chuffed**, cheekily.
"I am strong enough," he said. "I am Thomas and I pull the Express!"

Soon, Thomas was **puffing** around the Island. He had shown his guests some of the best sights, but he was starting to feel very tired.

"Gosh, the Express is heavy," he thought to himself. "But I can't let Gordon know I'm tired!" Thomas **chuffed** on.

By the time Thomas and the Very Important Visitors reached the Quarry, Thomas was nearly out of puff. Then he came up with an idea.

"If some of the visitors get off, the Express will be much **lighter**!" he thought.

"This is a very special sight," Thomas told the visitors. "I'll leave you here so you can have a good look!"

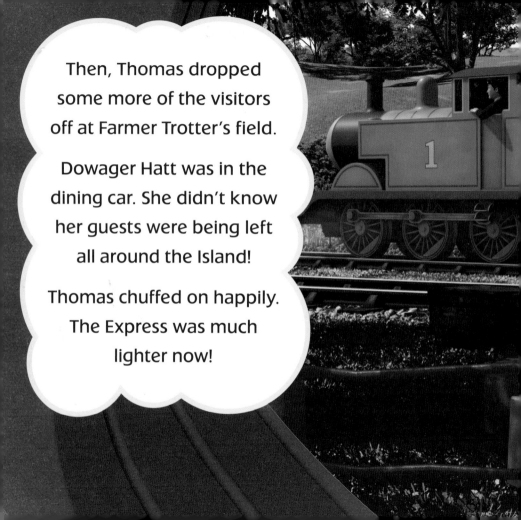

Then, Thomas dropped
some more of the visitors
off at Farmer Trotter's field.

Dowager Hatt was in the
dining car. She didn't know
her guests were being left
all around the Island!

Thomas chuffed on happily.
The Express was much
lighter now!

Back at the station, Dowager Hatt got off the Express. "Thank you, Thomas. That was a lovely ride around the Island. I do hope my guests enjoyed it."

Then she realised that her guests were missing!

"Thomas!" cried The Fat Controller. "Where are all the Very Important Visitors?"

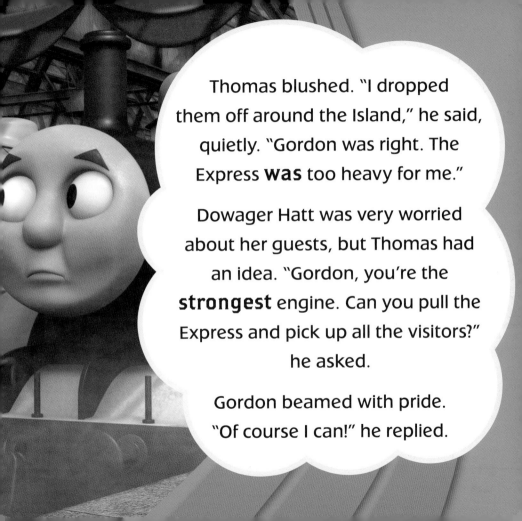

Thomas blushed. "I dropped them off around the Island," he said, quietly. "Gordon was right. The Express **was** too heavy for me."

Dowager Hatt was very worried about her guests, but Thomas had an idea. "Gordon, you're the **strongest** engine. Can you pull the Express and pick up all the visitors?" he asked.

Gordon beamed with pride. "Of course I can!" he replied.

Gordon collected all the visitors in time for a welcome party at the station. But Thomas was still feeling **sad** because he had been so silly.

"Where are all the balloons?" The Fat Controller **boomed**. "We can't have a party without balloons!"

The balloons had been left at the Docks!

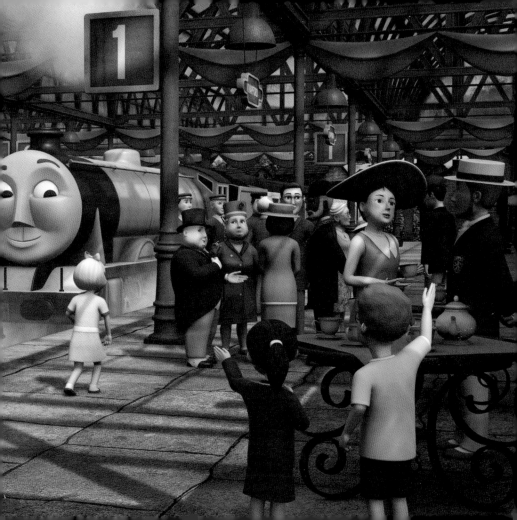

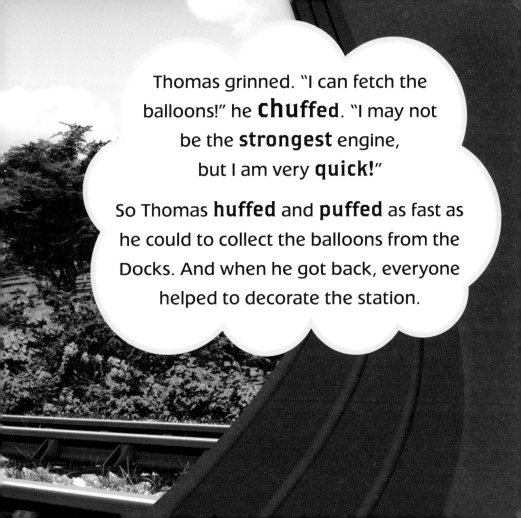

Thomas grinned. "I can fetch the balloons!" he **chuffed**. "I may not be the **strongest** engine, but I am very **quick!**"

So Thomas **huffed** and **puffed** as fast as he could to collect the balloons from the Docks. And when he got back, everyone helped to decorate the station.

All the engines and the Very Important Visitors were having a lovely time at the party. The Fat Controller clapped his hands for quiet.

"Welcome to the Island of Sodor," he began. "I hope you have enjoyed meeting my engines. Some of them are **really strong**. Some of them are **really fast**. But they are all **Really Useful!**"

PEEP! PEEP!

The End